JOEY AND JET IN SPACE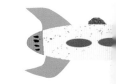

To my dad, who loved space shows,
and to Roger the Dodger

Atheneum Books for Young Readers • An imprint of
Simon & Schuster Children's Publishing Division • 1230
Avenue of the Americas, New York, New York 10020 •
Copyright © 2006 by James Yang • All rights reserved,
including the right of reproduction in whole or in part in
any form. • Book design by Polly Kanevsky • The text for
this book is set in Base 9 and 12. • The illustrations for
this book are rendered in digital pen and ink. •
Manufactured in China •   • 10 9 8 7 6 5 4 3 2 •
Library of Congress Cataloging-in-Publication Data •
Yang, James, 1960– • Joey and Jet in space / James
Yang. • p. cm. • "A Richard Jackson Book." • Summary:
When Jet runs away, he could be anywhere, maybe even
outer space. • ISBN-13: 978-0-689-86927-3 •
ISBN-10: 0-689-86927-4 • [1. Dogs—
Fiction. 2. Lost and found possessions—
Fiction. 3. Imagination—Fiction.] I. Title. •
PZ7.Y1934Joe 2006 • [E]—dc22 •
2005008237   1211 SCP

JOEY
AND JET
IN SPACE

James Yang

A Richard Jackson Book
Atheneum Books for Young Readers
new york london toronto sydney

This is Joey.

This is Jet.

They are outside . . .

. . . exploring space.

Jet sees his bone.

And he is gone.

Where IS that dog?

"Have you seen a dog?"

No Jet . . .

. . . anywhere.

Squeak!

"Joey! Jet!"

"Earth to Joey!
Earth to Jet!"

"Joey! Jet!"

"Time for lunch.

Squeak!

Even space explorers take time to eat